Best Friends
doodles

Buster Books

Illustrated by
Jessica Secheret

Edited by Hannah Cohen
Cover by Angie Allison

First published in Great Britain in 2010 by Buster Books,
an imprint of Michael O'Mara Books Limited,
9 Lion Yard, Tremadoc Road, London SW4 7NQ

A CIP catalogue record for this book is available from the British Library.

ISBN: 978-1-907151-14-9

2 4 6 8 10 9 7 5 3 1

This book was printed in July 2010 by WS Bookwell Limited, Teollisuustie 4, FIN-06100, Porvoo, Finland.

Papers used by Michael O'Mara Books are natural, recyclable products made from wood grown in sustainable
forests. The manufacturing processes conform to the environmental regulations of the country of origin.

www.mombooks.com/busterbooks
If you like doodling, visit our doodle website at: www.doyoudoodle.co.uk

Welcome friends!

This is your chance to celebrate friendship. The best friends you'll meet in this book love to do all the cool things you and your buddies enjoy doing together. So what are you waiting for? Grab some pens and join in the fun!

You can do these friendly doodles on your own or with chums. Design stuff for your 'BFF' (Best Friend Forever) and give her a picture present when you're done doodling.

True friendship lasts for ever, so get ready for a lifetime of fun!

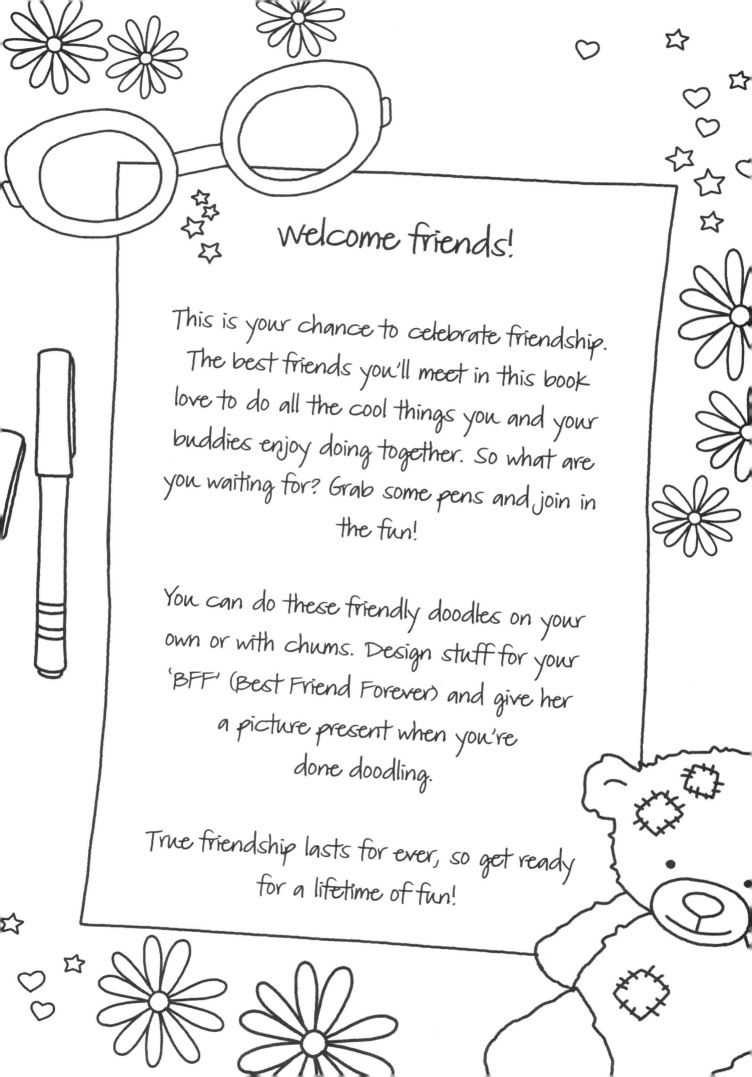

Make the friends' pyjamas gorgeous for a sleepover.

Beautifully

OTT

Random

CHiLDiSH

Design funky badges for you and your friends to wear.

what are the friends saving for?

Design a balloon for her BFF's birthday.

Give the fairy friends wings.

Decorate the friends' dresses for the fancy-dress ball.

Pamper the pal with a bath full of bubbles.

Design the perfect outfit for your best friend.

what would you paint for your pal?

Decorate the friends' umbrellas.

Design a team T-shirt for you
and your friends.

Design a beautiful birthday card
for your BFF.

what gift is she wrapping up for her friend?

Design three funky friendship rings.

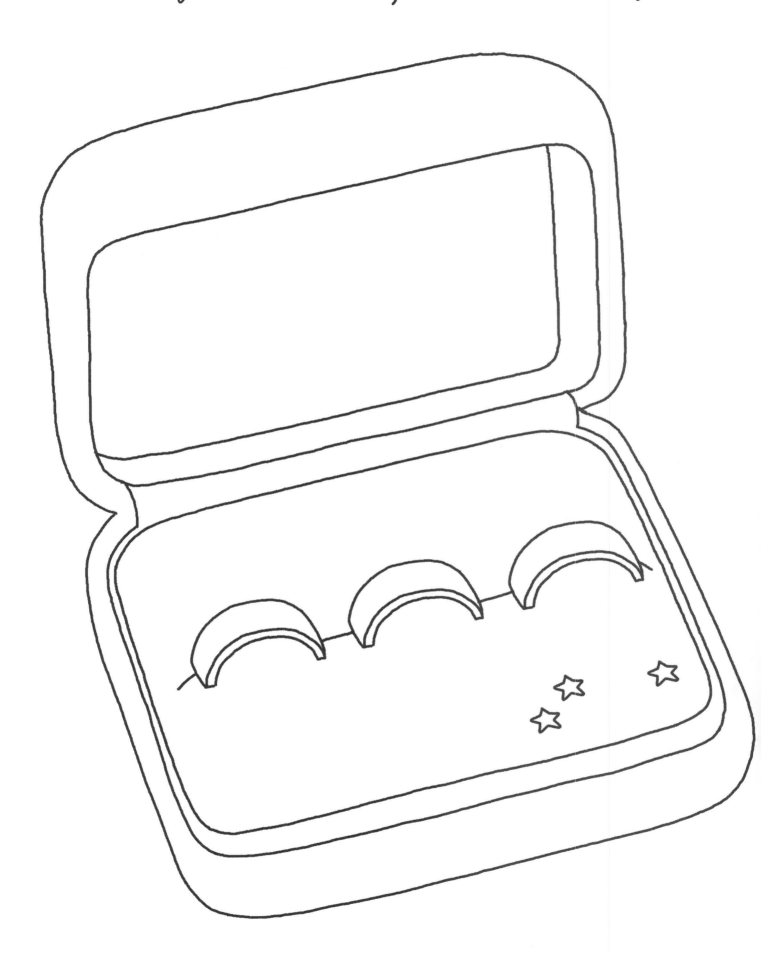

Give the girls their
'Friends Forever' rings.

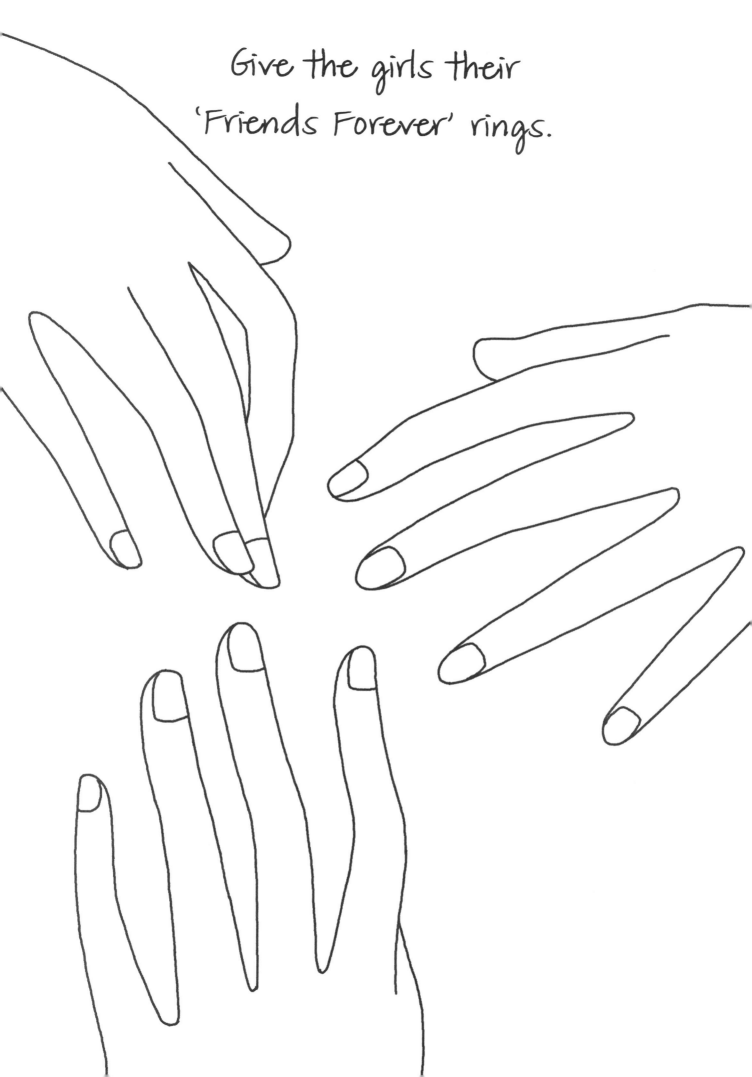

Give the mermaids tails.

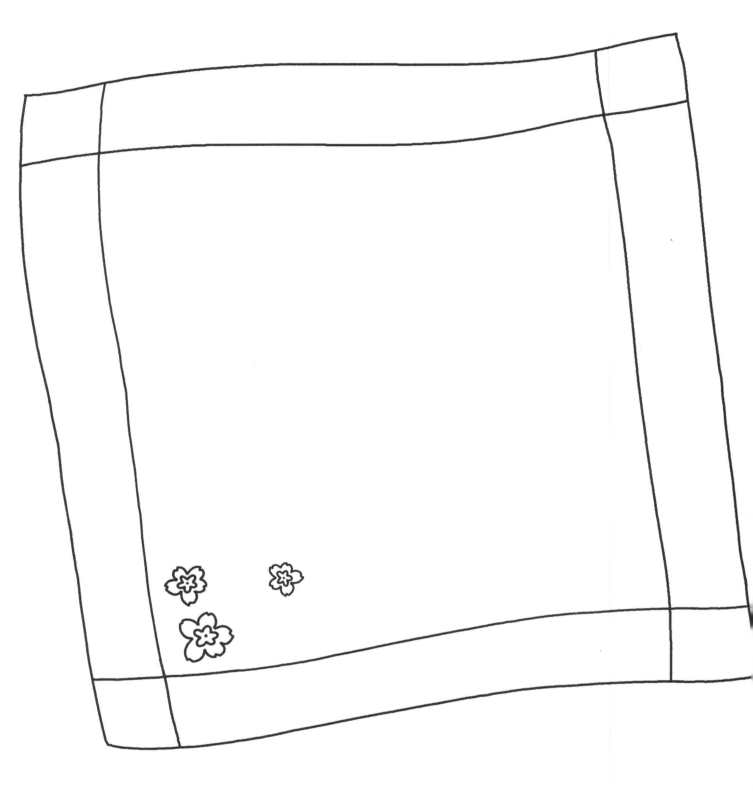

Design a pretty headscarf for a pal.

Decorate these best friends'
designer headscarves, too.

Give the friends cool skateboards to ride.

Decorate the birthday cake for your friend.

How many candles are there?

what is your best friend's favourite meal?

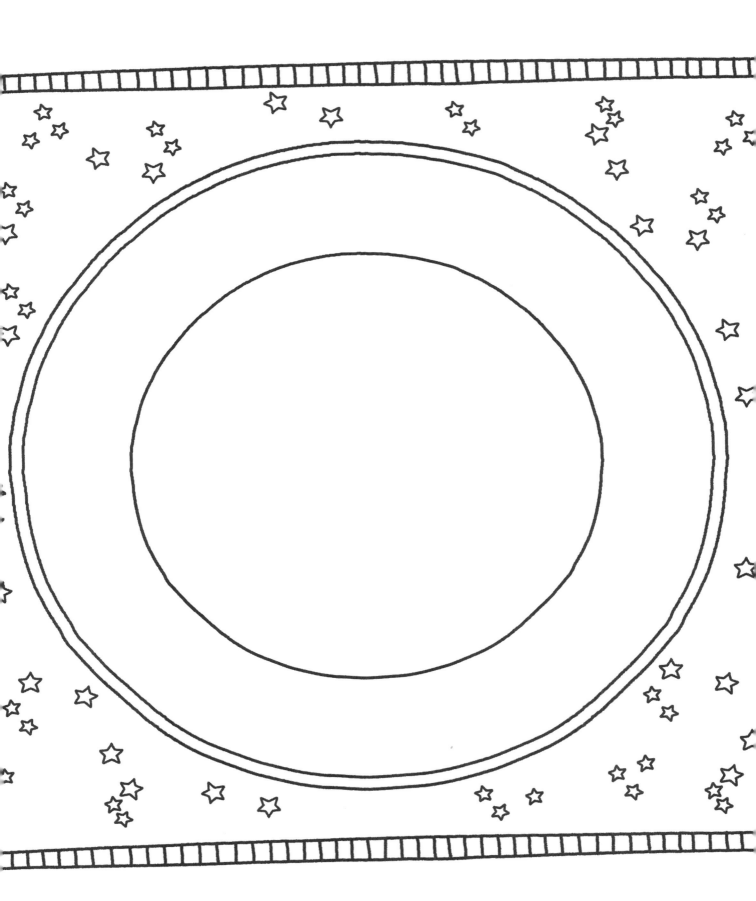

Snowball fight!

Design some pretty friendship charms.

Add more charms to the girls'
friendship bracelets.

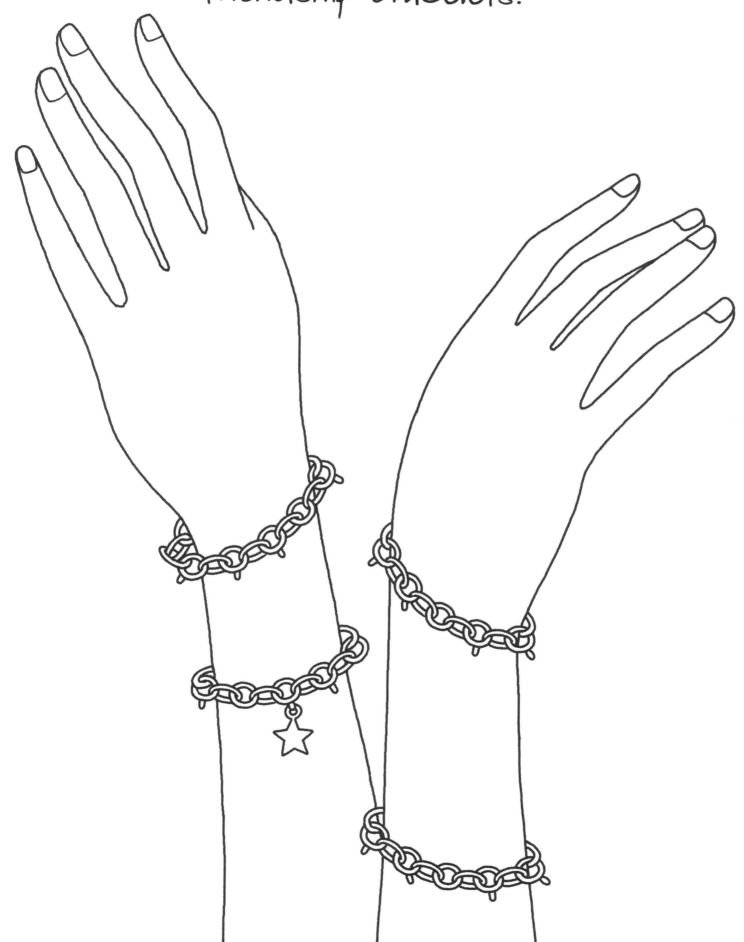

Design some cute toys for your friends to cuddle.

Give the cheerleader chums fluffy pompoms.

Add stars to their uniforms, too.

Best friends like nothing better than chatting for hours on the phone.

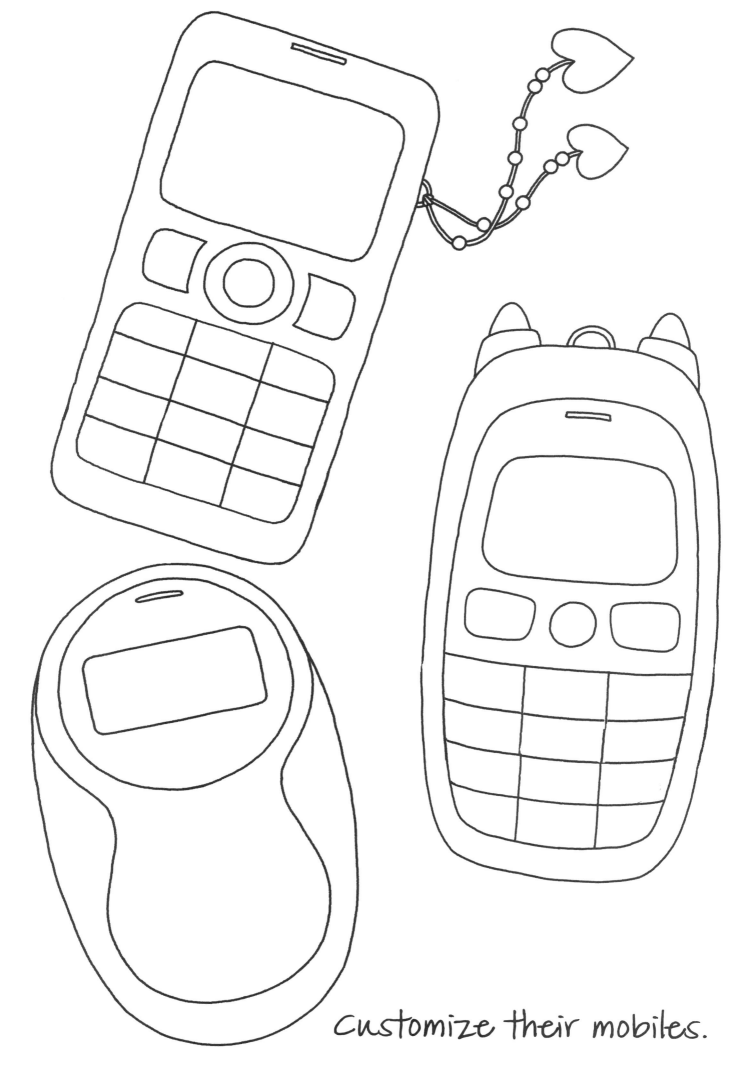

Customize their mobiles.

what is your best friend's favourite book?

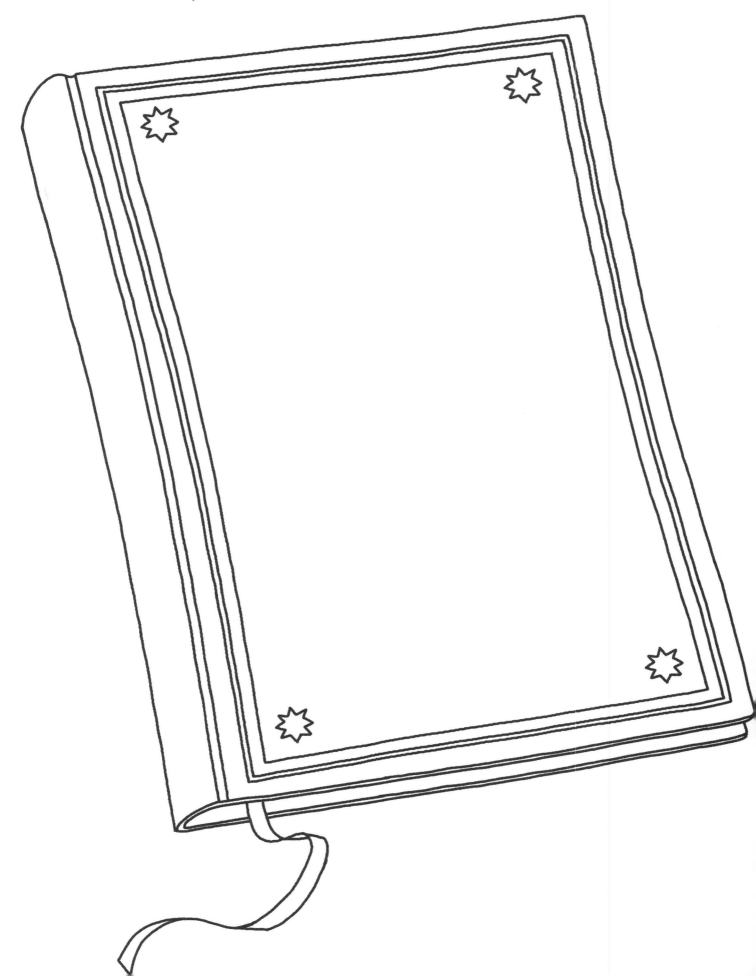

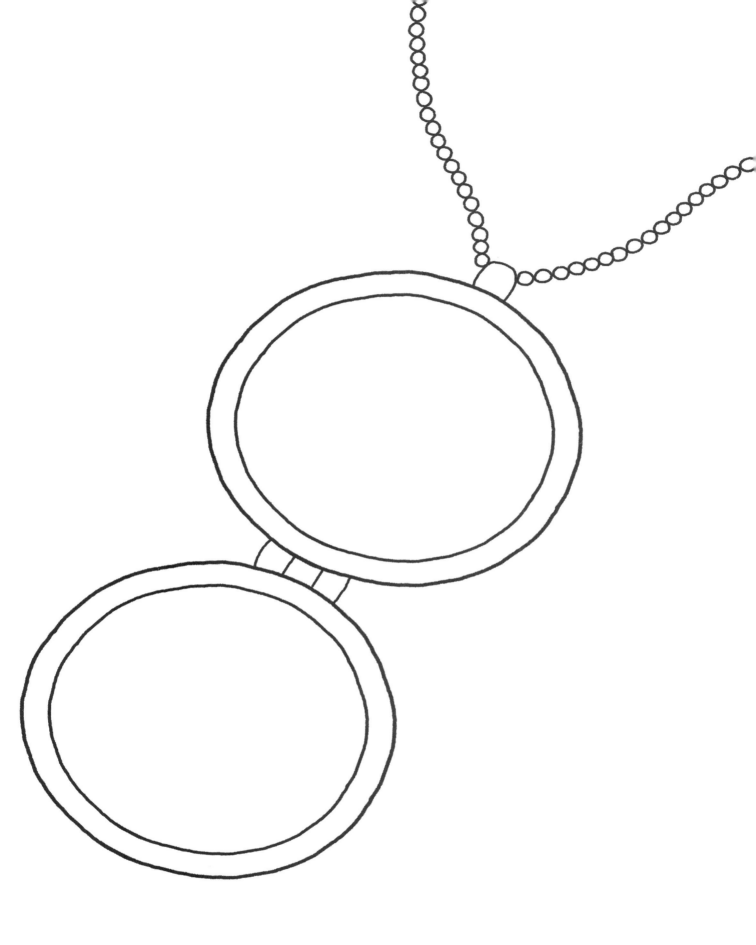

whose photograph is in this
friendship locket?

Best friends can read each other's thoughts. What are they thinking about?

what are they giggling about?

Add more popcorn to their bowls for the friends' DVD night . . .

. . . and give their sofa lots of comfy cushions to curl up on.

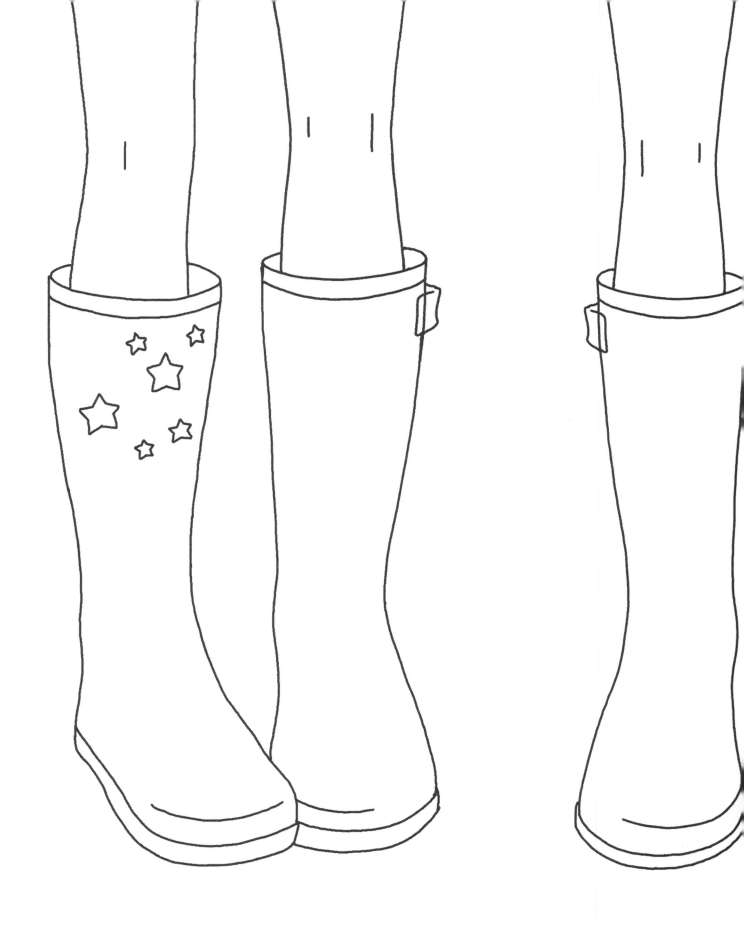

Friends are there for each other
come rain or shine!

Give these friends funky wellies so they can splash in puddles together.

Decorate the luggage for the friends' weekend away.

Design postcards for them to send to their pals back home.

The friends have been shopping.
Draw lots more shopping bags.

Stir up some exotic drinks for the friends to sip on a hot summer day.

Finish the friends' photo album.

Give the friends glamorous hairstyles at the salon.

If you had all the money in the world,
what would you buy your BFF?

Decorate the friends' swimming costumes.

Design their funky flip-flops.

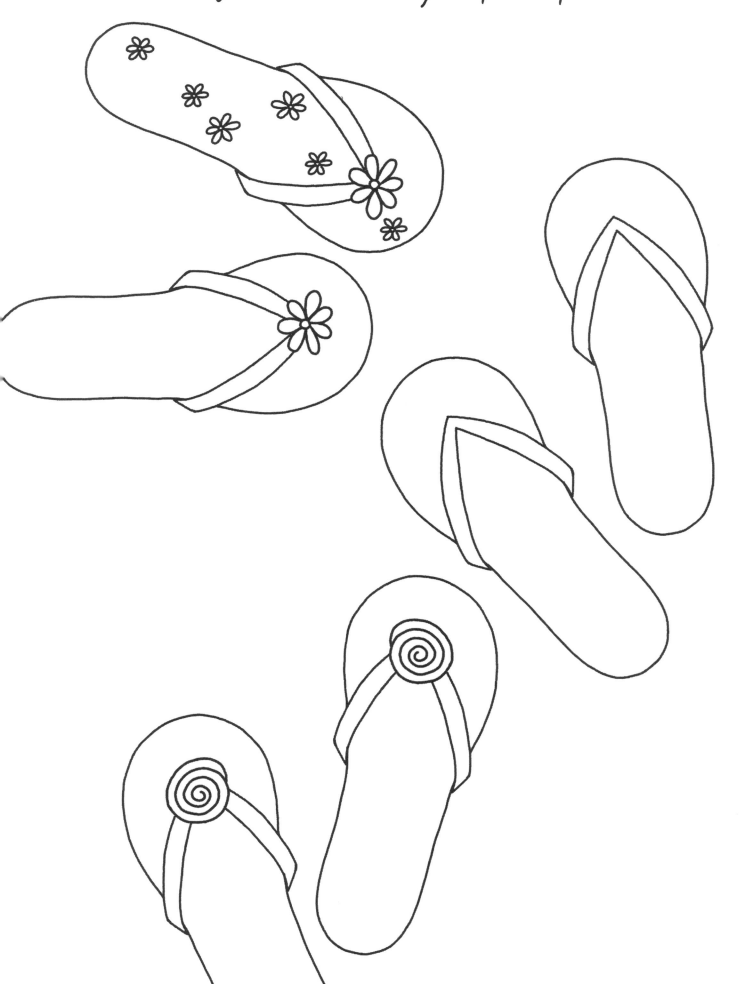

Design a friendship crest.

FRIENDS FOREVER

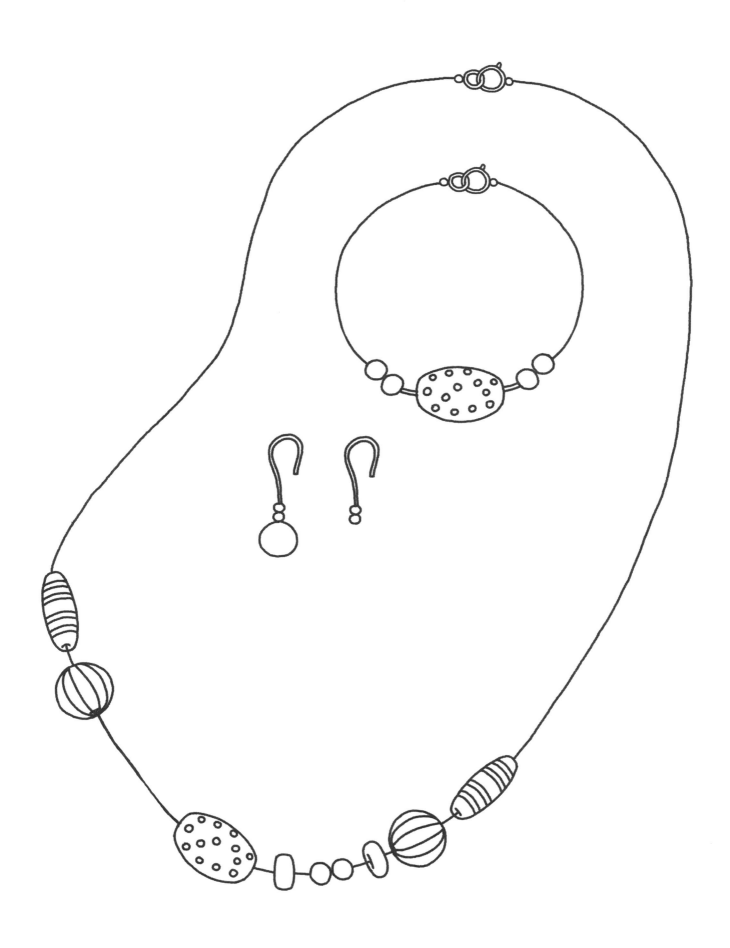

Design a jewellery set for your best friend.

Give the friends pretty pedicures and marvellous manicures.

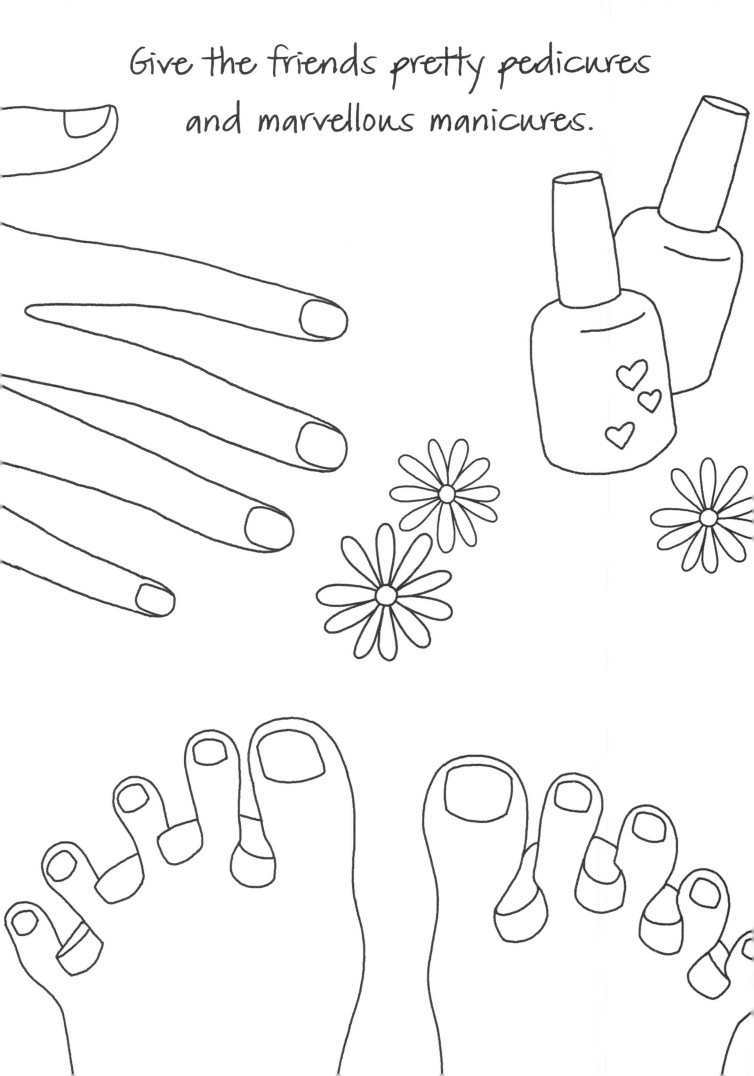

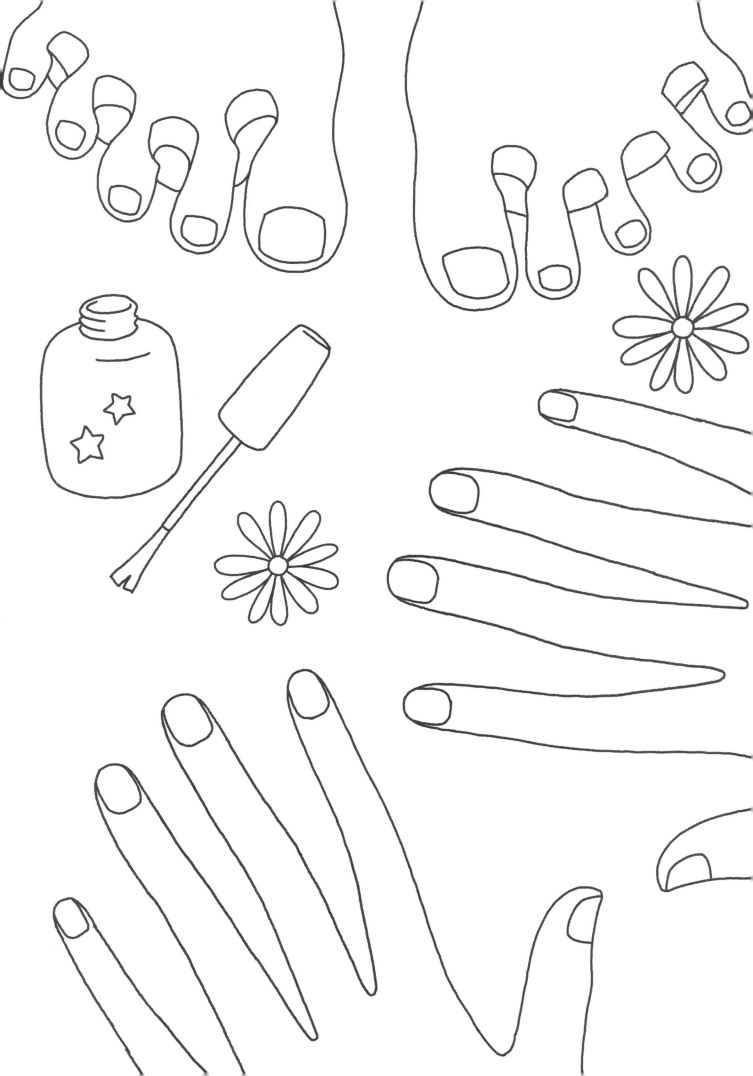

what treats are being served at the
teddy bears' picnic?

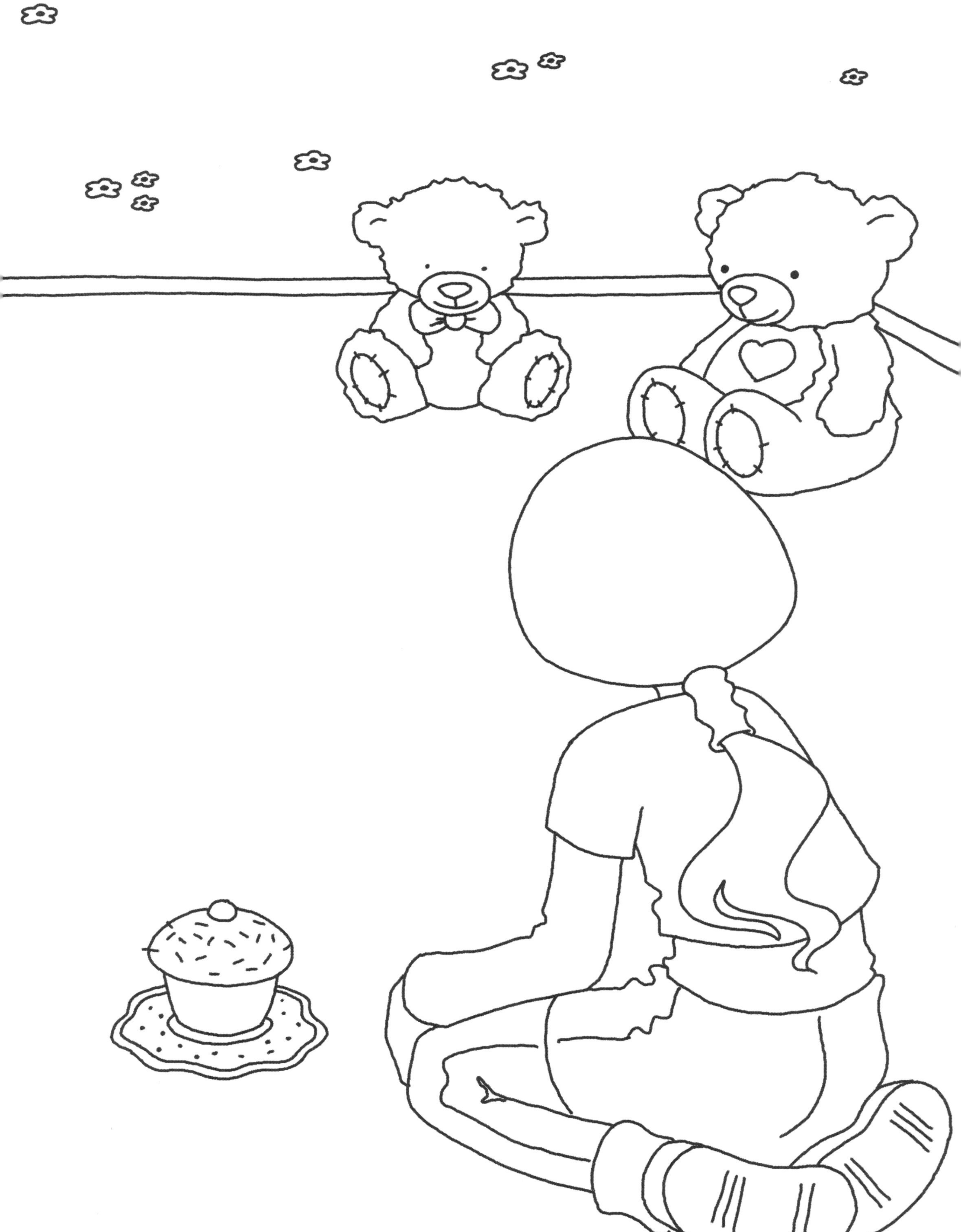

what have the friends got in their packed lunches today?

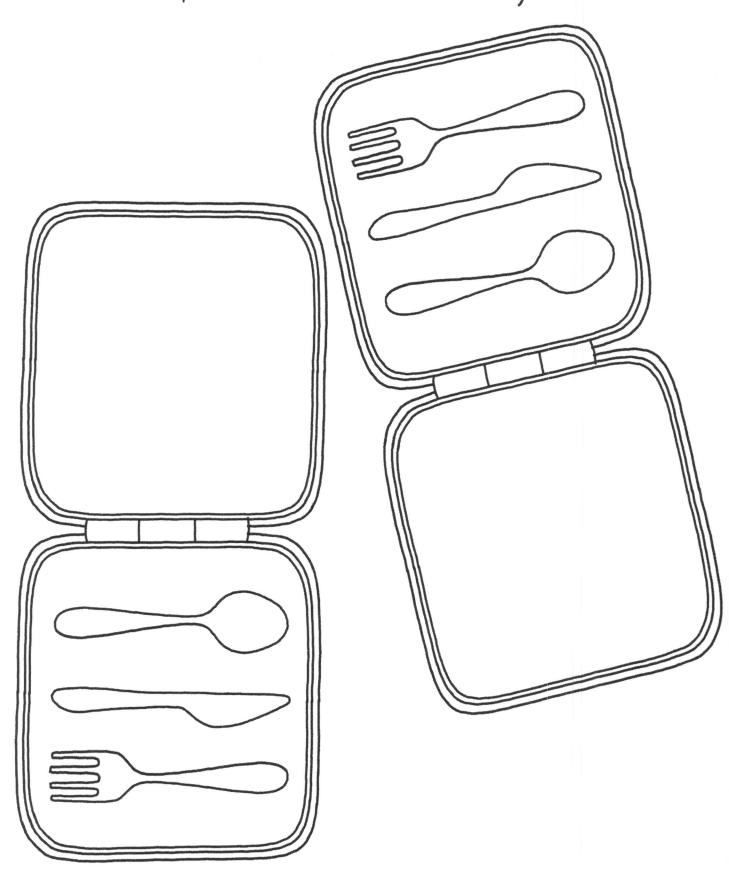

Finish the daisy chain for your best friend.

what's in the fridge for the friends' midnight feast?

Design a fabulous photo frame.

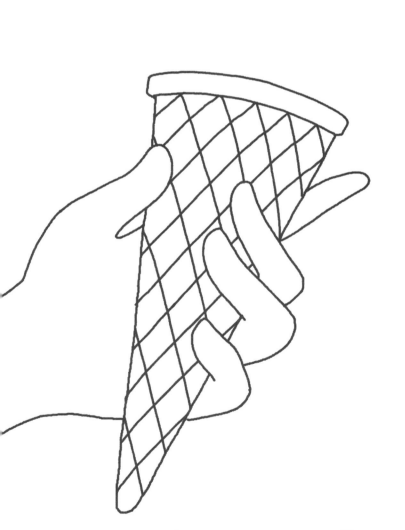
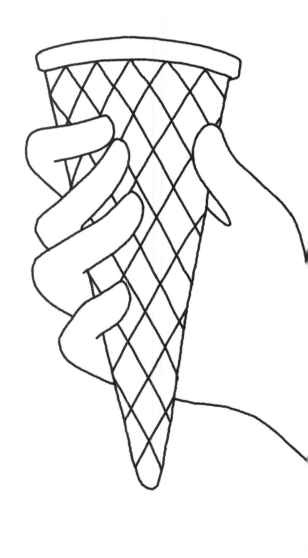

what type of ice cream do you
and your friend like?

Give the pizza toppings, and enough slices so all your friends can have one.

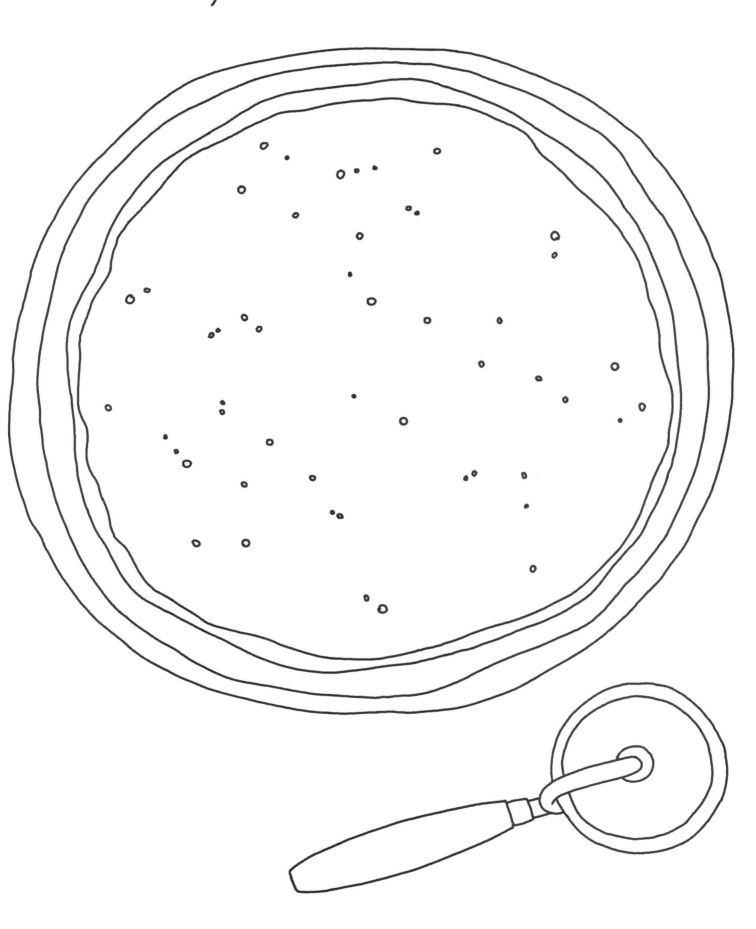

what is she planting in the garden?

what else has she grown in her garden?

Draw some friends skipping.

Dancing divas!

Give the friends funky leotards and tutus.

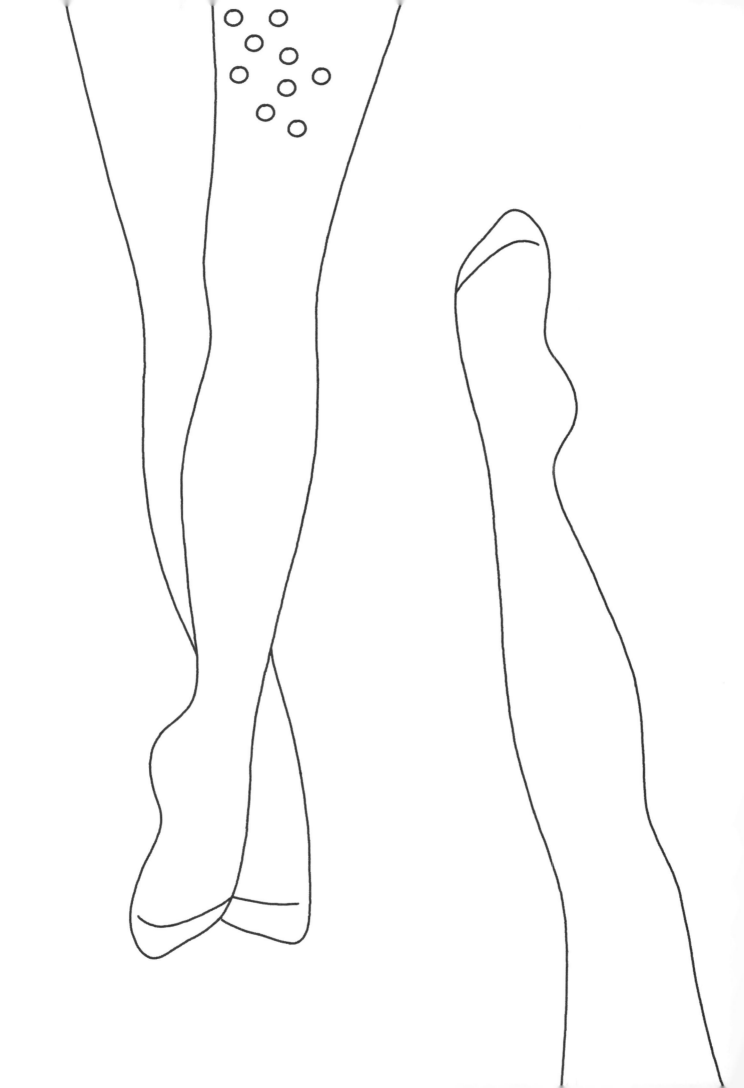

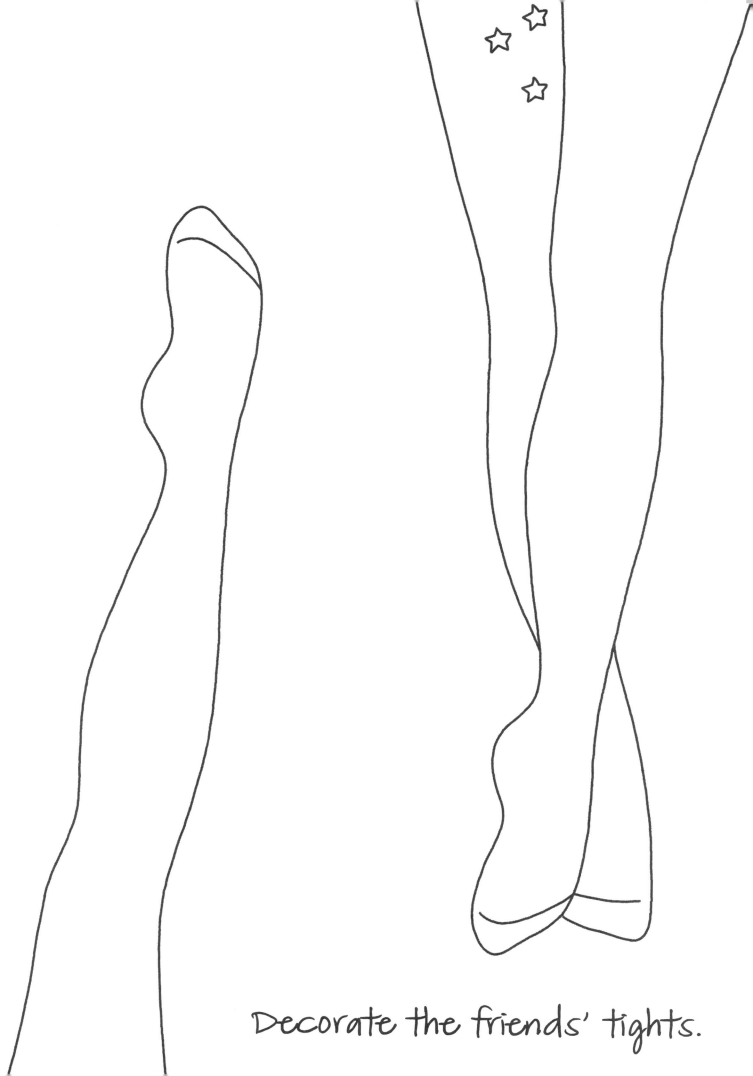

Decorate the friends' tights.

Give the friends funky gym wear for their exercise class.

The friends have put on a play.

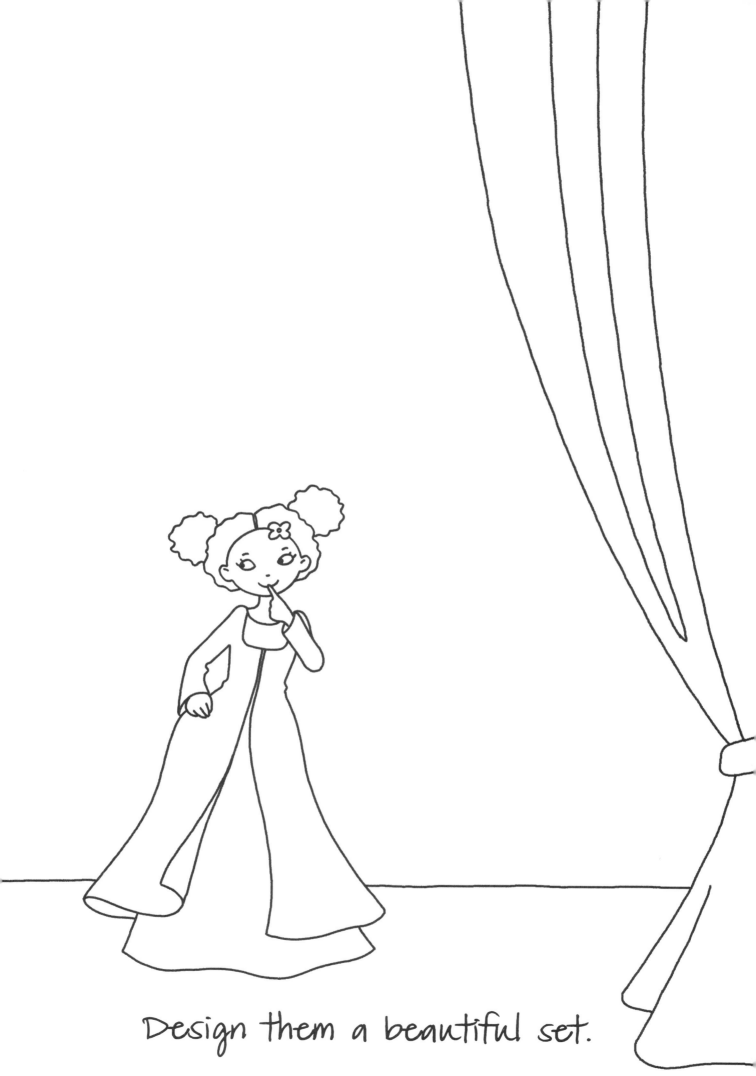

Design them a beautiful set.

Decorate the room for the friends' Halloween party.

Give them spooky witches' hats.

Seesaw!

Balance her with another friend.

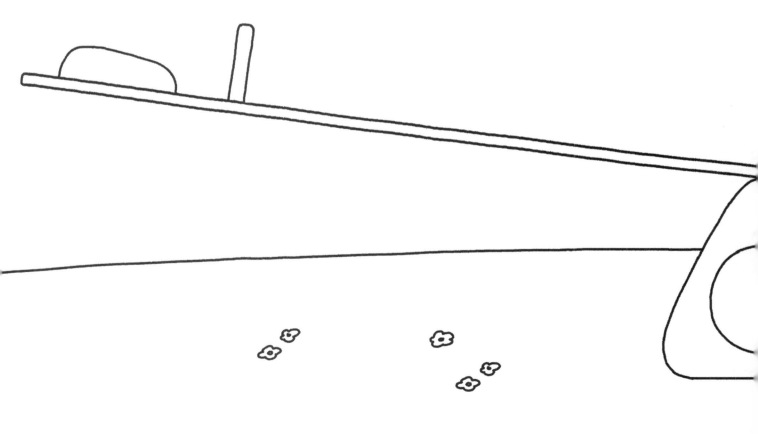

The friends are washing the car.

Cover them in soap suds.

Decorate the bouncy castle and draw
another bouncing chum.

what prize have the friends won at the fairground?

The friends are going to a party dressed
as superheroes.

Make their outfits super!

Give the friends pretty patterned towels to wear for their day at the spa.

Treat the chums to a strawberry and kiwi face mask. Finish the fruity wallpaper, too.

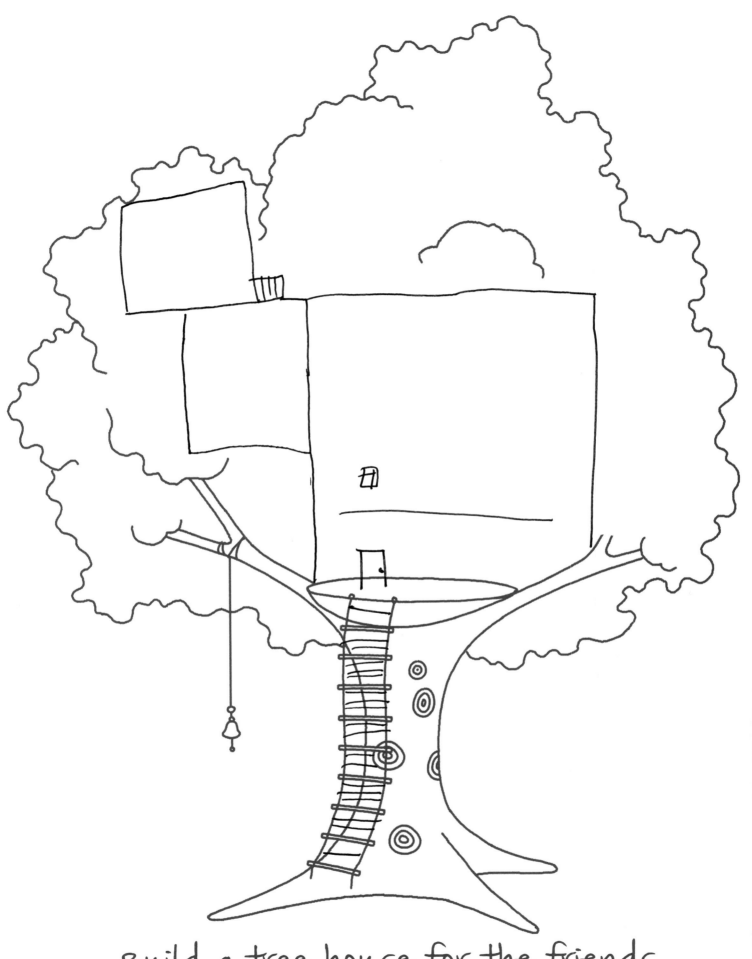

Build a tree house for the friends
to hang out in.

Make the inside cosy! Add more cushions
and put up pretty fairy lights.

Make friends, make friends,
never ever break friends.

Draw more friends linking arms.

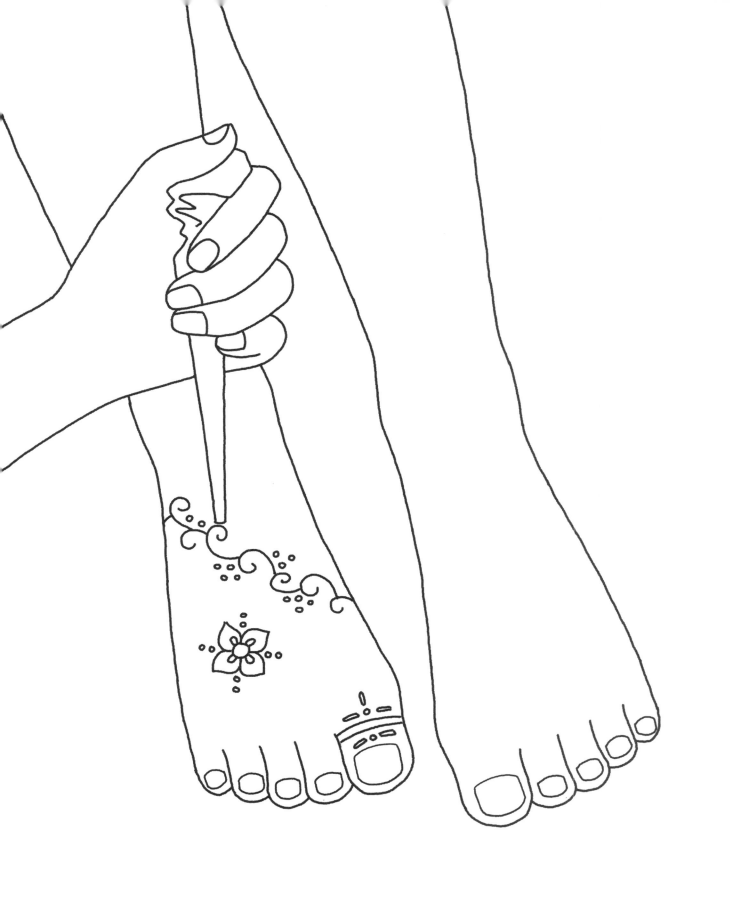

Finish the friends' beautiful henna tattoos.

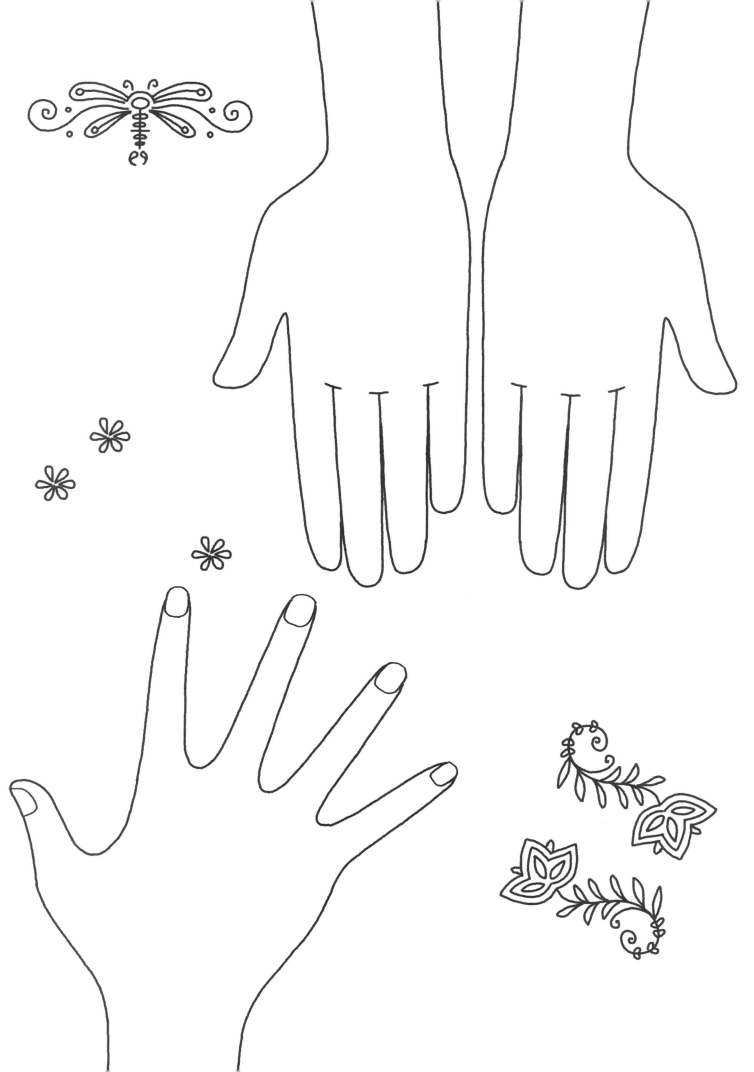

Best friends look after each other.

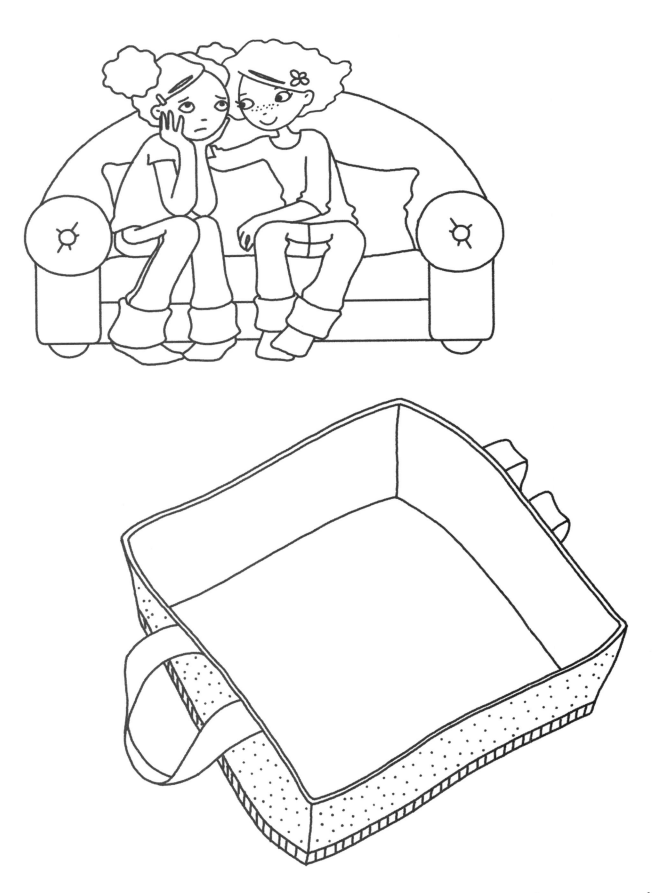

Fill the box with things to make her smile.

Create an ice-cream sundae to share.

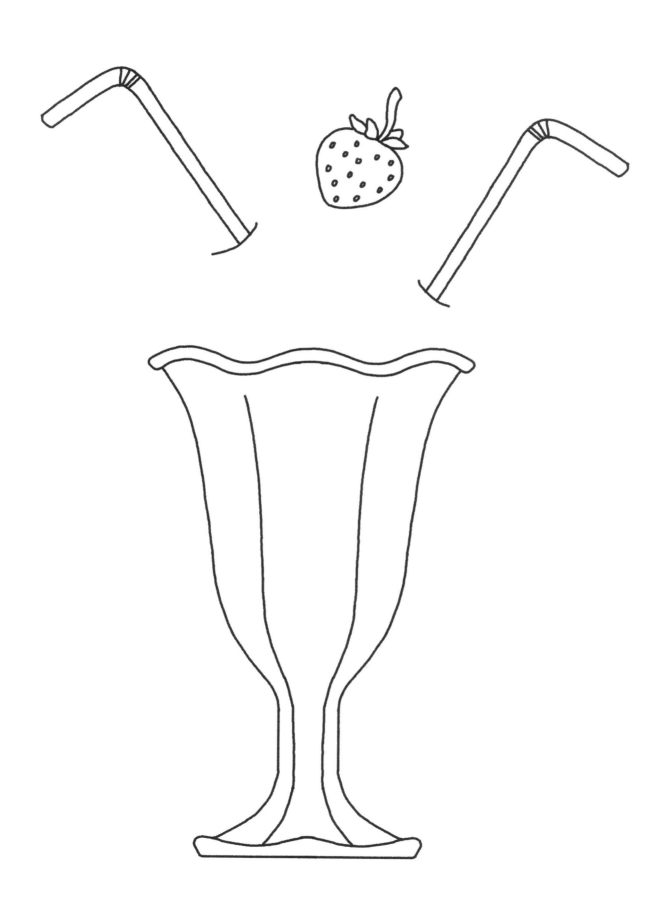

Draw more sweets in the jars for the friends to buy.

write a nice note to your BFF
on the chalkboard.

Help the friends finish the mural on the bedroom wall.

Fun on the pond!

Decorate the friends' sunhats and swimming costumes.

what delicious treats are the friends enjoying for afternoon tea?

So cute! Draw more animals in the pet shop.

Snakes and ladders! Finish the board.

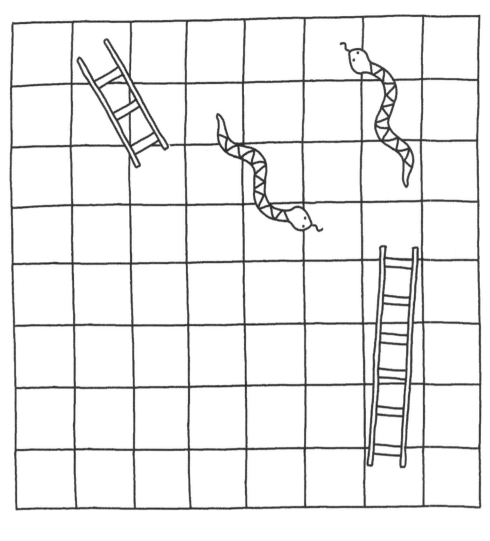

who is winning?

what did the friends bake for their sleepover?

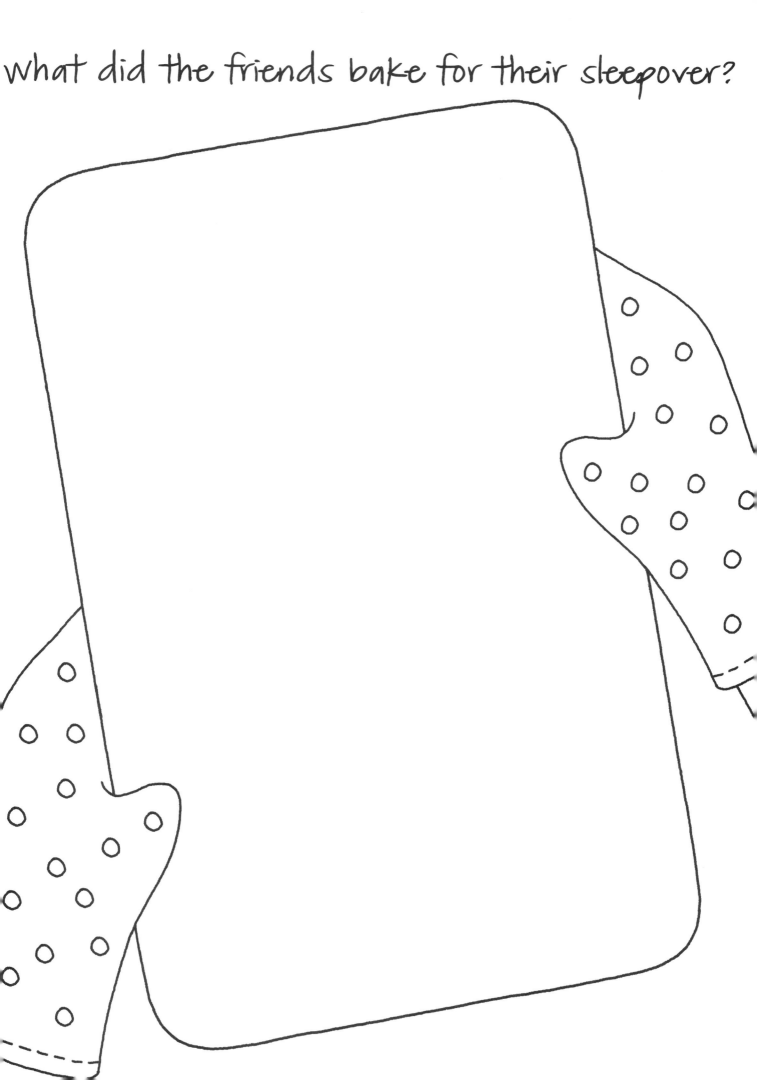

The best snowman ever!

The friends' band is going on tour.
Dress them in show-stopping outfits.

Design funky beach towels
for the friends to relax on.

Decorate the friends' rubber rings.

Pillow fight!

Give them pillows to throw and add plenty of flying feathers.

Give the friends flowery dresses for
a summer day in the park.

Add more ducks on the pond.

Camping trip! Decorate the friends' tents.

who's hiding inside?

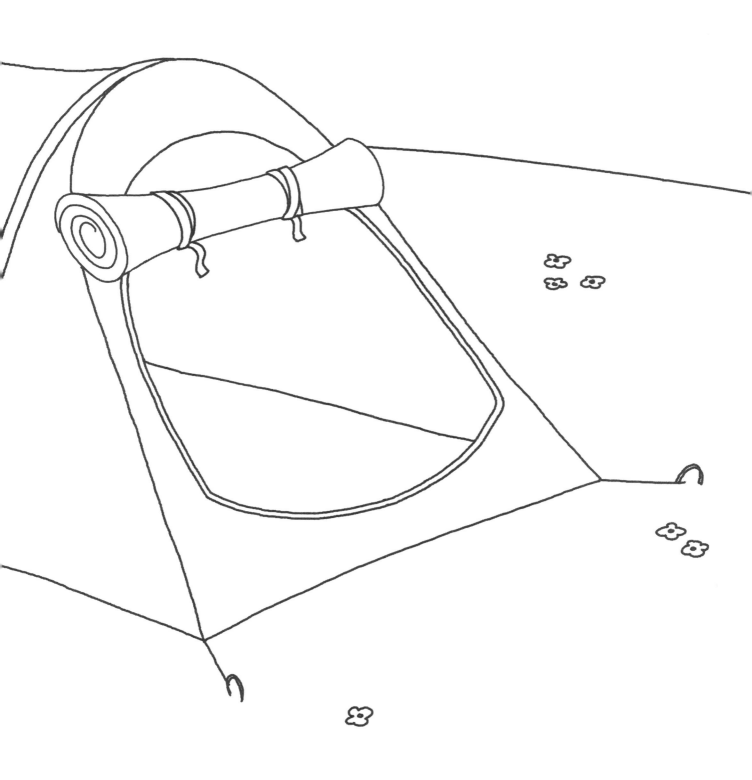

The friends have organized a car-boot sale.

what are they selling?

Pen pals keep in touch
with friends all over
the world.

Finish the pen pals' surroundings.

Even best friends have some secrets.

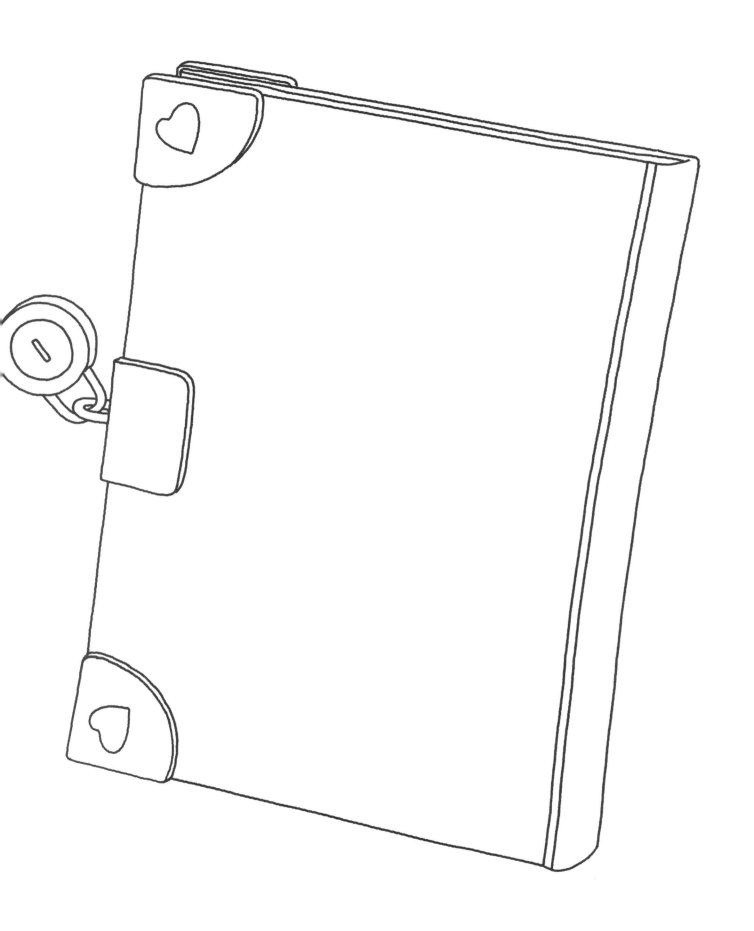

Decorate these secret diaries.

Complete the hopscotch grid for the chums to play on.

Draw more dogs for the friends to walk.

Design these biking buddies some
gorgeous helmets to wear.

Give their bikes pretty baskets, too.

what shapes can the friends see
in the clouds?

Draw more cloud shapes in the sky.

Draw the friends' speedy sledges and add more snowflakes.

Design funky sunglasses for the friends.

Give these surfer chicks cool surfboards to ride.

Give the friends amazing make-up.

NATURAL BEAUTY

RED-CARPET GLAMOUR

Give the friends matching outfits and some popcorn to munch at the cinema.

Make the friends' schoolbags stand out
from the crowd.

The friends are wishing on a star.
Fill the night sky.

Friendship should be treasured for ever.

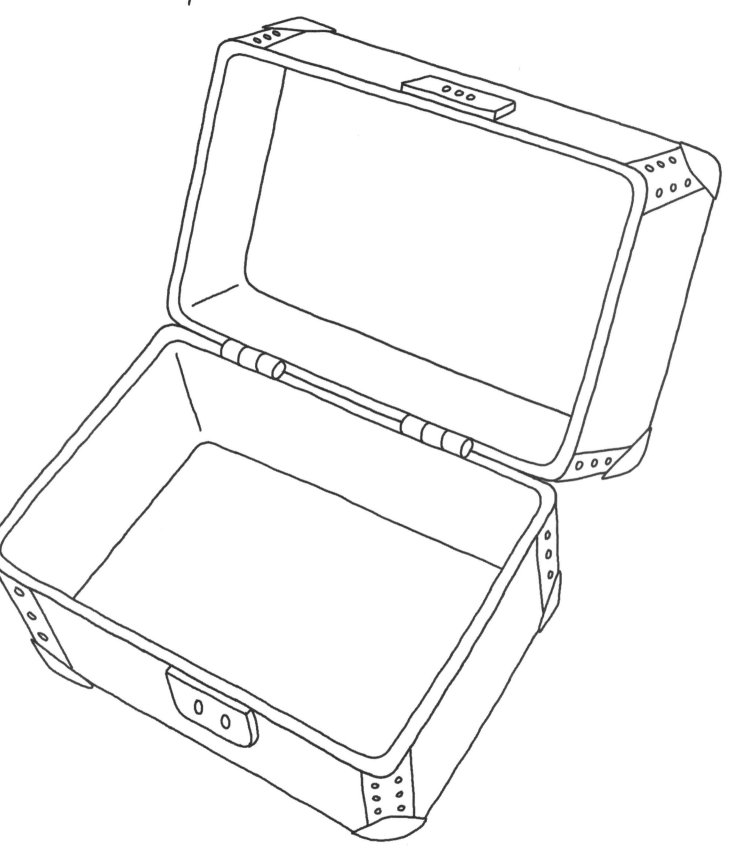

Fill this chest with your BFF's
favourite things.

Snorkelling is more fun with friends!
Give them snorkels.

Draw more
fish for them
to spot.

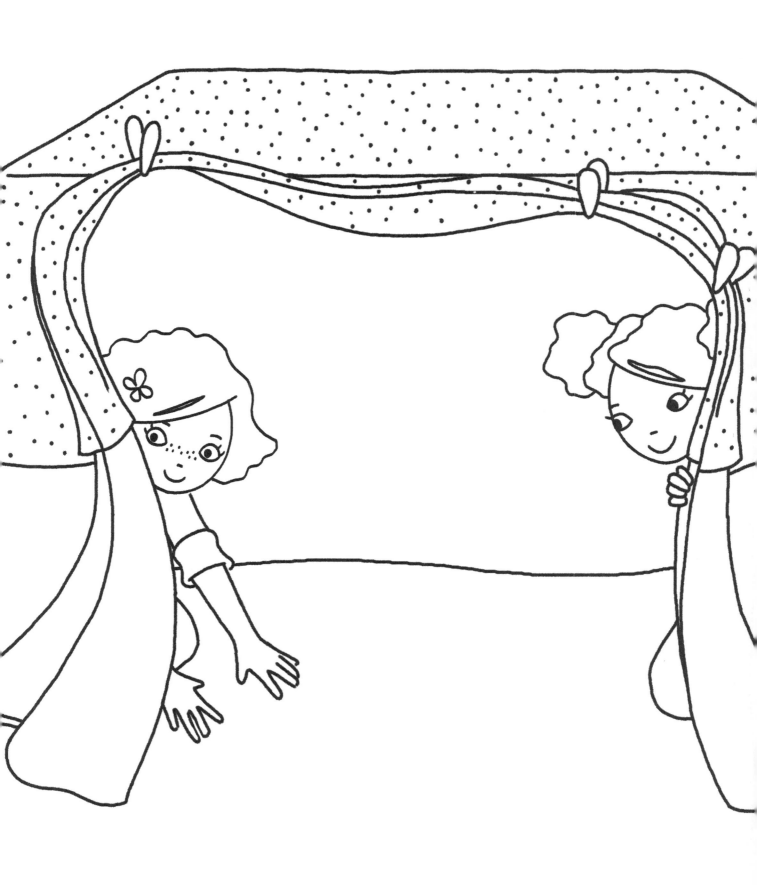

who else is hiding in the den?

Fill the patches on the quilt with pictures
of things your friends love.

Make these roller skates rockin'!

Give the friends cool outfits for
their roller-skating club.

Draw the horses' tails . . .

. . . and give the girls stylish saddles and hats.

Draw a friend on top of this pyramid.